RELENTLESS

BROTHERHOOD PROTECTORS WORLD

TINA DONAHUE

Twisted Page Press LLC

BROTHERHOOD PROTECTORS

ORIGINAL SERIES BY ELLE JAMES

They call him Ghost...

If anyone needs a hero, Nic does. Her grandfather died in a suspicious accident, she nearly lost the ranch to foreclosure, and now mysterious mutilations are killing her cattle. She suspects her supremacist neighbor is behind the crimes, but can't prove it.

When Ghost arrives on her land, offering to get justice, she's hard-pressed to refuse his help. He's sexy as sin and a former Army Ranger, his talents as a sniper unequaled.

The way he looks at her unmatched.

Ghost can't help himself. He's never met a more determined woman, her courage and intelligence captivating him. As a Blackfoot, he's always called Montana home. With Nic here, he's not going anywhere.

Good thing as the attacks escalate.

Facing insurmountable odds to save her land, Nic and Ghost form a formidable defense, while also surrendering to passion neither can resist.

ACKNOWLEDGMENTS

A special thanks to Elle James for inviting me to write for her Brotherhood Protectors series. I love her characters and those of the other talented authors who are expanding this wonderful world.

Also, thanks to Kate Richards' Wizards in Publishing and editor Laura Garland for her insightful edits. And to Nicole Austin for another beautiful cover.

CHAPTER 1

Nic Strom cradled her rifle beneath one arm and lifted an industrial lantern. Light streamed across the pasture, illuminating a dark, unmoving mass in the distance. Past it laid another object...or rather the remains from a second cow. A dead calf dotted an area to the right.

Her stomach churned, followed by white-hot rage.

Victor's never going to give up.

The powerful rancher had wanted this property for years, though not for its value. He didn't like her kind living in Montana. Nic believed he'd killed her grandfather to run her family off, though there wasn't any evidence to charge him.

To everyone's surprise, she'd saved the place, derailing Victor's plan. Now this.

Cautiously, she stepped forward.

Something crackled beneath her boot.

She flinched and snapped her fingers, wanting Shade, her black-and-white border collie, at her side.

The dog lifted his head to her, then sniffed the first carcass and stiffened, his attention drawn to something in the distance.

A low growl vibrated in his throat.

Nic lowered the lantern and brought up her rifle, prepared to shoot whatever SOB Victor had sent here. Motorcycle gang members and supremacists made up his preferred crew. Belligerents who thought their so-called pristine heritage and dicks made them the rightful rulers and God's gift to mankind.

Not on her damn turf.

Hackles raised, Shade snarled.

In the grayish dawn, a tall figure approached, shoulder-length hair flapping in the mild summer wind, the man's powerful form silhouetted against the lightening sky, his face hidden in shadows.

He carried a rifle over one shoulder.

Nic's fury morphed to dread at the coming battle, but she wouldn't back down. "Hold it right there!" Her shout sounded thunderous in the otherwise calm day. "Another step and I'll shoot off your balls."

Halted, he raised his hands. "I'm not here to cause trouble, Ms. Strom."

Patience and sincerity rang in his deep, rich voice, along with respect.

Her stomach fluttered in appreciation when it shouldn't have. Victor's men weren't close to civilized. Calling her a bitch or barking racial obscenities was more their style. Confused, she nevertheless kept her finger on the trigger, prepared to fire. "Then go back the way you came. Don't enter my property again."

"I'm here to talk. To help."

That made no sense. He couldn't be from the Sheriff's Department. Long ago, the law in this county proved they couldn't have cared less about her problems.

Teeth bared, Shade edged closer to the stranger and crouched, ready to pounce.

Slowly, the man lowered his arms. "How about I put my rifle on the ground then you call off your dog?"

Sounded reasonable, but she was long past what most would consider normal trust. In the distance, trees, bushes, and too much darkness hid countless dangers. "How many men did you bring with you?"

"None. It's just me, I swear. Trent asked me to come."

Stunned, she could barely speak. "My foreman?"

"Yeah. He and I were tight on the reservation before I left."

Trent was a Blackfoot, the same as her grandmother Kanti. That wasn't something a man working for Victor would admit to. Nor would Victor deign to hire someone with that lineage or anyone less than what he considered a real American…unless this was a new trick. Her skin grew clammy. "Trent didn't say anything to me."

"He wasn't sure you'd accept my help."

"Like roaming around my pasture in the dark among newly dead cattle? If that's the case, he's right. Put your rifle on the ground."

He complied.

So far, so good. "Shade, back off."

The dog maintained his threatening posture.

"*Now.*"

He whimpered and inched away.

Unarmed, the man straightened, hands at his side, palms facing her.

Curious, she lifted the lantern and approached, the light bathing him.

Her heart turned over.

She couldn't recall the last time she'd seen a more beautiful man, his age early thirties or so. Straight black hair and dark-brown eyes complemented his coppery skin and strong features. The scar on his left cheek enhanced his masculinity. Although lean, he owned a powerful form, a dark T-shirt and jeans hugging his firm muscles. Her pussy creamed, and there wasn't a damn thing she could do about it. "Besides being Trent's friend, who are you exactly?"

"Roy Ghost. I prefer Ghost to Roy." He offered his hand.

Shade growled.

"Quiet." She put the lantern on the ground then slid her fingers across Ghost's dry, warm palm, calloused from hard work.

Her legs weakened.

He gripped her hand firmly but gently, his behavior reassuring rather than threatening. "Can I call you Nic?"

Laughter bubbled to her throat at their civility, as if they'd just met in a bar and were getting to know each other, rather than standing in a field littered with dead cows. Reality killed her amusement. She brought back her hand and retrieved the lantern. "Trent told you about Victor?"

"Some. I'd like the full details."

Having suffered endless humiliation and worry over the years, plus losing her grandfather because of that maniac, wasn't something she wanted to relive. "The latest facts are over there." She inclined her head to the fallen cows. "You saw the carcasses, right?"

"Not closely. Carrying a lantern or flashlight gives away one's position."

Meaning hers, making her a target for whoever might be out there, watching and waiting. For some reason, she felt compelled to explain. "I was simply going about my chores as I do every morning. I wasn't trying to attract gunfire."

"Of course not. Nor should you have to worry about such things and won't from now on."

She wasn't following. "Trent offered you a job as a ranch hand?"

"No. I work for Brotherhood Protectors. Hank Patterson, a retired SEAL, established the ex-military group. We protect those who need our help."

The scar on his cheek appeared deadlier than before. "You were in the service?"

"Army Rangers, specifically a sniper."

His rifle glinted in the available light. She was a good shot, but next to what he could do... No wonder her threat hadn't alarmed him. "I can't pay for protection. I was barely able to save the ranch from foreclosure. Do you know about that?"

"Not the particulars, though I did catch your performances on *This Country Has Guts!*" His grin lit up his handsome features, making him more luscious. "Those motorcycle tricks were outstanding. You deserved to win the million."

Her smile happened before she could stop it. "Thanks. Bryce taught me."

"Bryce?"

"My grandfather." She lowered her rifle, realizing she'd still had it pointed at him, and hung the weapon over her shoulder. "He was a Hollywood stuntman before retiring here. What he called paradise until it turned into a never-ending nightmare." Pain swept through her, stealing her breath.

Ghost stepped closer, his mouth turned down. "You mean the trouble Victor's caused?"

"Trouble?" She shook from renewed outrage. "Try murder. He killed my grandfather. I don't know how he messed with Bryce's cycle, but he did. I called in the sheriff, but he claimed what happened was an accident. Bryce supposedly hit something on the range, and, given his speed, he flew off the cycle and broke his neck. The coroner accepted that as fact without any investigation. Hell, I had to fight for an autopsy, and, even then, they only did the bare minimum. They don't call this Victor County for nothing. Victor has every damn authority in his pocket. After the *alleged* accident, I'm sure he wasn't expecting me to keep this place up and running, which is why he's now killing my cattle." Hatred for him raced through her, tightening her shoulders. "You know what? Screw him. I'm not taking this another minute." She strode across the pasture.

"Whoa." Ghost caught her arm. "Where are you going?"

"To have this out with him once and for all. I'm tired of playing games. He wants a fight then I'll give him one he'll never forget." She yanked her arm.

He held tight. "That's not wise."

"I don't give a goddamn. Let. Go."

"Sorry, but no." He ran his thumb over her arm. "I don't want you getting hurt."

"It's my choice."

"That you'll regret. If you're dead next, who's going to run this ranch? From what Trent told me, you support yourself, your mother, and grandmother. What will they do if you're gone?"

Nic wanted to scream at him for mansplaining the obvious, but her exasperation evaporated into bone-deep weariness. Struggling for breath, she lowered her face. "I don't know how much more of this I can take."

"You shouldn't have to endure anything." He released her but eased closer, the wind delivering his subtle aquatic scent, clean and masculine.

Her pulse ticked up. She stepped back to keep from throwing her arms around his shoulders, begging him to hold her. For too long, she'd had to be strong and wanted only a moment to give into weakness, to have someone else take the burden. Wasn't going to happen. She was better than that. If nothing else, her mother had taught her to survive. "I know I shouldn't have to put up with this crap, but my feelings won't change what's happening."

"Then let's find something that will."

"Such as?"

Sunlight spilled over the horizon, illuminating the pasture.

He strode to the first cow. "Mind bringing the lantern over here?"

She positioned the beam to give them the best view and sucked in a breath. "What the hell?"

Rather than a bullet wound in the head, as she'd expected, the cow's right ear and eyeball were gone. Not gouged out or ripped off, but expertly removed, the jaw and tongue also missing. "What happened to the gore? Why didn't Shade hear anything? He's onto stray cats in a heartbeat no matter how far away they are."

Ghost hunkered down. "I don't know about Shade, though I wouldn't have expected any blood here."

"Are you serious? Why not?"

"This was made to look like the cattle mutilations in 2006 and earlier that everyone blamed on aliens. A good way to explain what happened so suspicion won't fall on Victor." Crouched, Ghost stared at the ground and pointed. "Shine the light over there."

She did.

He regarded the grassy area.

Shade padded close and sniffed the ground.

For once, Nic wished she had clothing from Victor's crew so Shade could match the scents on those fabrics to whatever odors were here. "Do you see anything?"

"A depression in the grass. Could be a boot print." Ghost pulled a smartphone from his back pocket and snapped pictures of this area then advanced, taking more shots.

She followed. "Is this the path his men took?"

"It stops here." He toed his cowboy boot against the ground.

"How is that possible?" She sank to her knees to look, but found nothing unusual. "They couldn't have taken wing and flown out of here."

"You'd be surprised what tricks people come up with to avoid detection." He returned to where they first stood, having taken care to step in the same areas he had previously. Eyes narrowed, he glanced at the gentle hills, fir trees, shrubs, and grassland, the cool air refreshing and fragrant, the utopia Bryce had loved so much.

Except for the mangled animals.

She matched Ghost's caution in not making additional shoe prints and stopped at his side, fighting an urge to press against him for safety and comfort. "Is someone out there?"

He met her gaze. His features softened and grew welcoming, interest then desire flaring in his eyes.

His reaction to her tangled Nic's thoughts. For the first time since Bryce convinced her she could trust him, she felt comfortable around another guy. Downright relaxed yet also excited. If her heart beat any faster, she'd black out.

"It's doubtful." His voice rumbled.

Heat suffused her. "What is?"

"It's unlikely his men would have stuck around to see your reaction." He offered a sympathetic look. "They did what they came for. I'm sure it's the only thing that matters to them."

She clutched his wrist. "Can you prove they did this?"

"I'll gather a team and have them check the

surroundings to see if his men left anything behind. Unless they did, there's no way to pin this on them."

That wasn't what she wanted to hear. "A team? I've already said I can't afford this. Three dead animals amount to ten grand or higher in replacement value. Add in the lost revenue from what they could have brought in and it's far more. This place is barely making it, thanks to what Victor keeps doing to us."

Ghost covered her hand, his warmth pouring into her. "I'd like you to tell me everything. And, please, don't worry about the cost. The Brotherhood doesn't do this to get rich. Consider our service pro bono. When you're back on your feet, you can make a donation to help others in your position."

"I can't… If I lose everything…"

"Believe me, I'm not trying to scare you, but things will likely get worse if you refuse my help. It's either settle this in your favor or let Victor run you off the land." Ghost squeezed her fingers. "Your choice. Tell me to leave or stay. I'll abide by whatever you want. No arguments."

Bryce was the only other man who'd shown such kindness and integrity. When he was gone, she'd believed such character traits had died with him. "What you're offering is too generous."

"Nope. It's pure selfish. I loathe people like Hal Victor more than you can imagine. It's time someone took him down." He shaded his eyes against the rising sun. "Is there somewhere we can talk?"

She wasn't certain if he despised Victor for what he'd done to her or if the man had hurt Ghost's family. "The house."

He collected his rifle, Shade padding after him. Ghost held out his hand for the dog to sniff. Once Shade had his fill, Ghost scratched him behind the ears. "Good boy."

She suppressed a smile. "He's supposed to tear strangers apart."

"Good. Thankfully, I'm not a stranger any longer." He joined her, bringing his heady fragrance and incredible warmth.

As a tall woman, few men could intimidate her with their height. Next to him, she felt positively dainty. Giddy, too. The way a shy teenage girl would react around the footfall captain. Rather than give into her emotions, she kept her cool. "I know your name, that you and Trent are friends, and you work at a protection agency. Other than those tidbits, you're a mystery."

"Yeah?" He regarded her mouth then her eyes, passion again sparking within his. "What else would you like to know?"

A man's voice shouldn't be that deep and soft, a dangerous combination to a woman's good sense and heart. Before she became too lost in his gaze, she squinted at the sun. "Why do you loathe people like Victor?"

"He's not an easy man to take."

"That's no answer, unless you know what he's like firsthand."

"Nope." He stroked Shade's head. "Never met the guy."

"But someone like him hurt you and your people on the reservation."

Caution and sorrow crossed his face, which he dismissed quickly, returning to his calm, collected demeanor. "In a manner of speaking."

He didn't want to talk about it, but she couldn't back off. If he was going to help her, she needed to know particulars, other than him being easy on the eyes and seemingly nice. Even a prick like Victor knew how to behave in polite society until he showed his true nature. "A white rancher bothered you?"

"No." He glanced at the distant mountains tinted bluish-gray in the faint light. "My white grandfather who held the same worldview as Victor when it comes to minorities." Ghost looked at her, his features hardened. "As far as Grandfather was concerned anyone who wasn't straight off the Mayflower was a loser and fair game to exploit. His golden rule. Like I said, a difficult guy to love. Where's your house?"

She felt awful for having brought up bad memories and wanted to console him for what he must have gone through given his mixed heritage. The right words wouldn't come. None would suffice for a child unwanted by their own blood and other people, the same as what she'd gone through.

Shoulder to shoulder, they walked the distance from the pasture to Bryce's log cabin. What he'd considered homey, but the locals referred to as Hollywood rustic. The two-story structure bore a wide porch, manicured lawn, trimmed bushes, and countless flowers.

Shade bounded ahead.

Nic clamped Ghost's forearm, stopping him.

"I don't know how much Trent told you about me and my family, but we're not typical."

He shrugged. "Who is?"

She chuckled. "I get that everyone has an obnoxious Uncle Dave or crazy Aunt Carole, but Bryce and Kanti, his wife, adopted me and my mother. We're not their blood."

His dark eyebrows lifted slightly. "You *and* your mom?"

"She was twenty-one at the time. I was five." Ordinarily, Nic wasn't one to share her horrible past with anyone, but he was different. As he'd said, no longer a stranger. "She escaped her boyfriend, my father—I won't call him a dad, he was never that. If she hadn't fled, he would have beaten her to death then turned his rage on me. When we got to town, we were dirty and starving, looking to find anything to eat in the supermarket dumpster. The sheriff back then ordered us to leave his county. The other upstanding citizens stayed clear and glared, as if we contaminated their pure surroundings. When Bryce and Kanti left the store, they saw what was going on. They were the only ones who offered to help, giving us food, shelter, and a family. A blood bond could never be as strong as what I feel for them. So, don't act surprised that we don't look like each other, in the least, and don't say anything to upset Kanti or my mother. They've been through enough. They don't need to know the gory details about the cattle, just that some have died and you're here to help find out what happened."

"I am. Until you tell me to go."

Honesty showed on his face, sincerity ringing in his voice.

Relieved not to be alone any longer, yet unsettled as to whether she was doing the right thing, she gestured to the porch then rushed toward it.

CHAPTER 2

GHOST SHOULDN'T HAVE STARED at Nic's ass but couldn't help himself. Her firm cheeks mesmerized him, the same as her tight jeans, long legs, slender yet athletic build, and lovely face.

She put her lantern on a step then looked over at him, her gaze questioning as to why he hadn't followed.

Walking wasn't something he could do right now. He guessed her to be mid-to-late twenties, her exotic features part African American, part Caucasian, her complexion a delightful cinnamon color. She wore her wavy brown mane parted in the middle. The sun or a hair-coloring product had produced the gold-streaked locks on either side of her face, the tint matching her feathered earrings. Her eyes were surprisingly light for hazel, her mouth lush, lips begging for a kiss.

She gave him a look. "You coming?"

A loaded question he didn't want to answer, considering how his dick strained against his fly, wanting out and into her sweet, heated cunt. He nodded and joined her, warning himself not to stare at her boobs.

Too late. Her hard nipples pressed against her white T-shirt.

She turned from him and climbed the brief stairway.

Still reeling, he followed.

Heavenly bacon, bread, coffee, and other breakfast scents embraced him the moment he stepped through the front door.

"Nic?" A woman's voice called from another room. "Is that you?"

"Yeah, Mom." She put her rifle on a side table. "I brought someone with me."

Plates and silverware clattered. "Is he or she staying for breakfast?"

Nic gave him the once over, settling on his chest and groin, the erection he couldn't hide. Her cheeks turned bright pink. She glanced away. "Looks like it." She leaned toward him. "Even if you're not hungry, eat something." She spoke softly. "Do not hurt her or Kanti's feelings."

"Never."

Relief crossed her face.

He guessed she'd expected him to argue with her. What man would over something as small as making her mother and grandmother feel good?

Her father, that's who.

The prick they'd escaped from.

His initial belief about Victor causing her skittishness around men had been dead wrong. Her father started her on the road to distrust. The one man who was supposed to have protected her above all others had instead posed the greatest threat, until she and her mother arrived here. Then they'd had to contend with Victor and his deadly crew.

Anger pulsed through Ghost at what she'd suffered over the years. No more. Victor wasn't invincible. He was a little man owning an even smaller mind, and by God, if it took Ghost's last breath, he'd bring him down.

She took his hand.

His face and chest heated, his remaining blood pouring into his groin, stiffening his cock.

"Hey." She edged closer and stared at his eyes. "What's wrong?"

He wanted to kiss her until the day ended and bury his dick in her pussy clear to dawn then start over again. "Nothing."

"Your face is red. Either you're pissed or you're blushing. Which is it?"

Rather than tell her what he'd been thinking, he opted to lie. "Neither. My complexion is always this color. Remember me saying I know Trent from the reservation?"

"Fine. Don't answer. However..." She released his hand and poked his chest. "If my mom or Kanti ask you anything, you don't dodge, understand?" She flicked her wrist. "Unless it's something they shouldn't know."

He enjoyed her soft, melodious voice and having her close. Her fresh, light scent smelled like the air after a gentle rain. "As in the dead cattle?"

"Exactly...and other things."

"Such as?"

"I don't know right off. But the moment a subject comes up that you shouldn't answer, I'll kick you under the table. Let's go. Wait." She stopped him before he could take a step. "No need for them to see this." She touched his rifle.

He delivered the weapon to her and waited as she placed it on another long table. Comfy leather furniture and brass lamps populated the space, giving the room a masculine feel softened by a female touch—a colorful afghan on the sofa, pillows boasting sage maxims. A huge stone fireplace took up one wall. The rest had floor-to-ceiling windows. Not a good thing for avoiding snipers.

His gut twisted. Surely, Victor wouldn't be that brazen. The cattle thing was a surprise but understandable since a story about aliens mutilating the herd could cover up his crime. But to outright kill Nic or the other women here…

"Hey, again." She squeezed his fingers. "What's wrong?" She stared at the windows as he had, worry flickering in her eyes. "Did you see something strange out there?"

"No. Do you always keep the blinds and shades open?"

"Sure. We don't have any neighbors who might peek in on us."

He cupped her shoulder, surprised at how

small she felt. "Until we settle things, the moment you turn the lights on, I want you to hide this room and the other areas from the outside."

Color drained from her face. "Are you saying his men might shoot us through the windows?"

"I'm asking you not to tempt fate. As soon as I pull a team together, I'll have them set up armed patrols at night."

"Nic, food's ready." Her mother sounded relaxed and happy.

Ghost intended to keep her that way.

"Bring your friend in." More plates clattered. "Don't let your meal get cold."

"Go on." He eased away from Nic and pulled out his phone. "I'll be there in a few."

The moment she left the room, he called Hank. "Hey, got a thorny situation on the Caldwell ranch in Victor County."

Something squeaked on the other end of the line, possibly Hank's chair. "Let me guess. That prick Hal Victor is using the Caldwell ranch to graze his cattle and claiming that's his right?"

"I wouldn't doubt it, but this is far more serious." Ghost detailed the cattle situation and Nic's take on her grandfather's death.

Bryce Caldwell's portrait hung over the mantle. He'd been a handsome man, silver streaking his dark hair, laugh lines around his blue eyes, face and neck tanned from too many days in the sun, his shoulders and chest burly, befitting a stuntman.

Finished bringing Hank up to date, Ghost wound down.

Hank whistled through his teeth. "What do you need?"

"All the men you can spare to patrol the area at night and a crew to check out the pasture ASAP to see if we can find any clues that will nail Victor and his men."

"I'll start on it immediately."

"Thanks. By the way, Nic Strom—she's Caldwell's granddaughter—doesn't have the funds to pay for this. She nearly lost the ranch until she entered that reality show *This Country Has Guts!* If she hadn't won, her property would be on the auction block, Victor buying it for pennies on the dollar. I told her we'd help. Take my pay, if you want. It's only money. I can't tell her no. I can't leave her unprotected against—"

"You're preaching to the choir. Whatever you and she need, you got it. Our entertainment clients can make up the difference. God knows, they should do something worthwhile with the bucks they have."

"Thanks." He ended the call and entered the kitchen.

Shade stood next to the stove, tail swishing, head raised to a sixty-something woman scooping scrambled eggs from a cast-iron skillet onto a platter, her hair white, complexion tawny, features pure Blackfoot. Had to be Kanti, Bryce's wife.

An African-American woman in her early forties took the eggs from Kanti and placed them, butter, and a jar of blackberry preserves on the table, her skin black as night, curly hair close-cropped, her features so beautiful she could have been a model in her day—except for the long, cruel scar marring her forearm. Its pinkish sheen proved the injury occurred years or decades earlier. Possibly from her boyfriend who'd tried to kill her.

Kanti and Nic's mom stared at him, exchanged a glance, then looked at her.

She stopped pouring orange juice. "Mom, Kanti, this is Roy Ghost. He prefers Ghost to Roy. As our new hire, he's going to help Trent with…stuff." She gestured between the women and him. "Ghost, this is my mom, Zara, and grandmother, Kanti."

He offered his hand. "Nice to meet you both."

They shook hands then looked at Nic worriedly.

No one had to tell him they hadn't bought her evasion about the "stuff" he did. She didn't want them upset, but to leave them in the dark concerning Victor wasn't wise either. They could walk into something and realize too late there was no escape. The same as what happened with Bryce. "Nic, they have to know."

She bristled until they glanced at her. "About your work? Why? It's just regular stuff."

"No, it's not." He hated to go against her wishes, but there wasn't another choice. "I'm here to stop Victor from trying anything else on the ranch or with any of you."

Kanti sagged to a chair.

Zara plopped in another. "What has he done now?"

"Nothing." Nic massaged her mother's shoulders. "And he won't. Ghost worries too much." She bared her teeth at him. "Don't you?"

He pulled out a chair and touched her arm. "Please sit, so we can discuss this."

"I'd rather not."

"I understand where you're coming from, but if they don't know what's been happening, I can't protect them. Neither can you. Caution will keep everyone alive."

Kanti pressed her hand to her throat. "What are you talking about?"

Although Ghost should have eased into this matter more judiciously, he couldn't turn back now. "It's no secret Victor wants you off this ranch. I don't know what lengths he'll go to in order to get his wish, especially since Nic's winnings saved it." Despite her glare, he soldiered on. "Trent called me yesterday, regarding the problems here. We go way back, and I said I'd help." He explained about the Brotherhood Protectors and their mission. "We can't waste time. This morning, three cattle are dead. I need to know details about what else has been happening."

The women looked at Nic.

Kanti spoke first. "What happened to the cattle?"

Ghost jumped in before Nic offered a lie.

"Someone on Victor's crew mutilated them. I'm here to stop that from happening again, but I need your help."

"Of course." Zara gestured him to sit then patted Nic's hand. "Stop trying to protect us. We need to know what we're facing."

"I'll handle it, Mom. You've been through too much already."

Zara fingered the scar on her arm. "I'll live. Now sit."

Once Nic had, he settled in his chair, Shade at his side, tail still swishing, eyes pleading for food.

Nic tossed a pet store package to Ghost. He offered Shade a doggy treat and stroked his head as he spoke to her. "Tell me every wrong Victor's done to your family or anyone else."

She sipped her coffee. "That would take days."

"I have all the time you need." He offered his gentlest smile.

Blushing, she grabbed a biscuit and focused on buttering it. "Victor hasn't paid grazing fees for years even though other ranchers, which include us, have done so. The last I heard, he owes the feds over a million dollars."

Ghost scooped eggs onto his plate. "No one's called him on it?"

Kanti leaned forward. "He's been in and out of court for years. Those judges constantly rule against him, but that doesn't change anything. He still puts his cattle on land he has no right to and never pays for what they take."

"Why should he?" Nic spooned preserves on her biscuit. "He owns everyone in the county who's worth owning. Sheriff Rettner refuses to do anything to upset him. His detectives and deputies are the same. Since Victor schmoozes with local judges and funds their reelection campaigns, they're not about to bite the proverbial hand that feeds them. He has every supremacist and motorcycle gang member in this state on his side. They're his posse. No way is anyone messing with Victor while they're around. Hell, they're just itching to kill someone who's not like them. Victor's even had the gall to graze his cattle on the reservations, saying his ancestral rights give him preference over people who were here long before his ilk ever darkened the shores. He's special, don't you know?"

Ghost did. All his life he'd known people like Victor who wanted America for their kind, the chosen masters of the universe. Currently, they bitched about Hollywood liberals taking over

Montana. They might have grudgingly ignored Bryce because he was at least white, but for him to marry a Native American must have goaded Victor. Then for him and Kanti to adopt a black woman and her mixed-race child had to have set his teeth on edge. "Has he tried to graze his cattle on this ranch?"

Nic rubbed her forehead. "Worse."

"You mean he's killed your cattle before now?"

"No."

Zara touched Nic's arm. "Show him. He needs to know."

On a heavy sigh, Nic left her seat and returned holding a binder, papers stuffed inside to the point the cover barely closed. She placed the lot near Ghost's plate.

He touched the vinyl cover. "What is this?"

"His lawsuits against us." She took her seat. "Unending motions, depositions, court appearances, you name it, it's there."

This he hadn't expected and opened the binder, the first date surprising him. "Is this in chronological order?"

The women nodded.

Victor had been suing Bryce, Kandi, and then

Nic and her mom for years, claiming the property to the south was his—by ancestral right—stating his great-great-great grandmother was actually a Blackfoot...or Crow, Cheyenne, Dakota. The tribes and land he demanded for his own kept changing over the years. Once a judge dismissed his latest lawsuit, he started another and another, unendingly. "Why hasn't anyone stopped him from filing this nonsense?"

Nic squeezed her fist, her face reddened, gaze murderous. "They need money either for reelection or other matters. Victor has it. He gives them what they want, and they stay out of his way until they have no choice but to rule against him or risk being overturned by a higher court, which no judge wants."

"But this is still nuts." Ghost closed the binder. "None of these suits had merit."

"They don't have to." Zara wrung her hands. "They've accomplished what he wanted from the outset. He knew he'd never win. He simply wants to take our time away from the ranch, force us to hire attorneys and spend our money on fighting him, rather than maintaining this place. Before Nic won the contest, he'd nearly bankrupted us with his last suit. He said he's not giving up until we turn over the land to him."

Nic spoke through her teeth. "Never. I'd die first."

"No!" Zara cupped Nic's face. "Don't ever talk like that. If anything happened to you, I'd…" She covered her eyes.

Hugging her, Kanti looked at Ghost. "He killed my Bryce, didn't he?"

Ghost would have bet his life on it. "I intend to find out."

"Then what?" Nic threw up her hands. "Bryce was white, and this is private property. There's no federal crime involved to get them to do anything, not that they would since they let his cattle graze for free, no matter what a judge says. How do we stop him?"

"Together." Ghost cradled her fingers, hating how icy they were, wanting nothing in her future except safety and hope. "We'll be as relentless as he's been, until there's no longer a threat."

CHAPTER 3

BUOYED by Ghost's confidence and determination, Nic allowed herself to relax, hope brightening her mood.

Hours later, her optimism was long gone as deputies *finally* rolled up in their official car. Throughout the morning and afternoon, she'd made numerous calls to the Sheriff's Department, repeatedly begging for someone to investigate her mutilated cattle.

The two young men viewed the carcasses dispassionately, neither one taking notes, photos, nor interviewing anyone on the ranch as to whether they'd seen or heard anything.

Her patience thinned further. "Aren't you going to do something?"

The redheaded deputy toed the dead calf. "We don't haul off carcasses. Have your men handle it unless you'd prefer to pay animal control."

She wanted to slug him. Ghost's loaded glance warned Nic to keep her cool. She dug her nails into her palms and tried her best. "I don't want you to remove them. I'm asking you to *please* investigate the slaughter."

The other deputy looked at his watch. "Not much we can do about an alien attack."

Good God, this is the Twilight Zone. Renewed frustration stung her skin. "Victor's men did this. Everyone knows he's been trying to run me and my family off this ranch."

Deputy Redhead narrowed his eyes, his hand resting on his holster. "You best be careful what you say. We don't take lightly to people slandering honest folk in this county." He elbowed his partner. "Come on. Nothing to see here."

Refusing to give up, she called the Sheriff's Department again and pleaded her case as calmly and humbly as she could. "Please tell Sheriff Rettner TV crews will be out here shortly because of the unusual mutilations. For him to be on hand and publicly comment as to his department's handling this case would be great publicity for his reelection campaign."

Ghost laughed softly but did wag his finger at her.

She grinned and ended her call. "If that doesn't get the fool out here, nothing will."

Within the half-hour, Rettner sauntered onto her land, his gaze darting in every direction. She supposed he was looking for the TV people. Not seeing any, he glared and strode toward her, his beer belly leading the way. "Why didn't you tell the reporters to hang on? I got here as fast as I could."

Far quicker than he'd arrived for Bryce's murder investigation. "Sorry, but I don't handle reporter schedules." She gestured to the cattle. "Please investigate what happened to my herd. We have photos of depressions in the grass and cigarette butts from the men who did—"

"We do *not* handle alien attacks." He pivoted to leave.

She hurried around him and stood in his way. "Victor's men did this. We found butts from their smokes. Their DNA is surely on the filters. You'll have that as soon as you test them." She held up the plastic baggie containing the evidence, found earlier by Ghost's team.

Rettner pushed her hand away. "Like I said, we don't investigate attacks from space creatures we can't arrest. I've got real crime to see to."

Although she would have given a decade of her life to kick him in his shriveled balls, she strained for control. "You're not going to do anything about this?"

He looked down his nose at her. "I can't manage the impossible."

"What about an autopsy to determine what caused the animals' injuries?"

Laughter quivered his flabby throat. "The coroner only works on humans. You'd have to call a vet for what you want. I recommend the animal hospital."

Owned and operated by Ethan Victor, Hal's first-born. Ethan employed every vet in the area, his monopoly having destroyed any animal doctor who was crazy enough to compete against his and his daddy's power. "That's your honest advice?"

"Don't offer it any other way."

Besides being lying scum, he'd missed her sarcasm.

He glanced to either side, dung dotting the grass. His only choice was to step in it if he wanted to get past her.

She didn't budge.

"Look, I don't know what even a vet can tell you." He scratched his neck, sending his cowboy hat bouncing. "Except the obvious."

His cryptic comments made her teeth hurt. "Such as?"

"Ain't no flies on the carcasses. A pure sign of an alien attack."

Precisely what she'd read in the news stories Ghost had showed her. "Or a chemical compound to keep insects away to make this look like something it's not and hide the real perpetrator's crime."

He gave her a blank look. "Can't help you with that."

"So you keep saying, but what about my losses?" She jabbed her thumb at the carcasses. "Those animals represent thousands in lost revenue."

"Yeah, that's a real bitch, ain't it?" He shrugged. "If you were wise, you'd look on the bright side."

"Meaning?"

"Call the *National Enquirer* or one of them other tabloid magazines. I'm sure you'll make good money selling your story to them. It's a perfect solution for your kind."

Her heart quickened, sending blood to her face. "My what?"

He regarded her as he might manure stuck to his shoe. "You like being the center of attention, like when you were on that fool TV show. Now you got your chance for more publicity, like them trashy Kardashian girls. As far as this nonsense goes…" He gestured to the cattle. "Do not bother me or my department again, unless you want me to arrest you for trying to file a false report."

He made a wide circle around the droppings and lumbered to his car.

Ghost caught her arm, keeping her from following Rettner and kneeing him. "Don't." His mouth grazed her ear, his sweet breath warm against her cheek. "He's not worth it."

A protest rose in her throat stopped by tears stinging her eyes. "I despise jerks like him."

"I hear you, but he can't stop justice forever. Nor can Victor." Ghost eased back. "It's getting late."

The sun hung low in the sky, dusk approaching. She'd waited the entire day for the sheriff and his men to arrive only to dismiss and humiliate her. No different from when Bryce was murdered. "Are you going on patrol with your team?"

He nodded.

"I'm coming, too."

"No." He grasped her shoulders lightly. "It's best you stay with your mom and grandmother. I'm sure they'd like to know what's been happening."

As if she'd be cruel enough to repeat what the law had said or how they'd treated her. "Will you be careful?"

Already she worried about his safety and losing him...saying goodbye when this was settled or when he and his employer couldn't afford to fight Victor for free any longer. She didn't want to consider how many days it would take for such a thing to happen. Weeks weren't even in the equation. The only sure thing was how she'd ache at his absence. "Promise you won't take any unnecessary chances."

His dark eyes glittered in the waning light. "I

never have." He released her. "Do you still have the motorcycle Bryce rode the last day?"

"It's in the garage. Why?"

"I'd like you to show it to me tomorrow morning and the area where he went down. Can we do that at seven or so?"

"Sure. But won't you need more sleep if you stay up all night?"

"Once my men have everything under control, I'll turn in at an appropriate hour." He smiled. "The guesthouse you set up is too nice for me to ignore."

She'd changed the bed linen and cleaned like a maniac to make the place perfect so he'd have no excuse to leave the property. "If you need anything tonight, please don't hesitate to come to the main house. I'm a light sleeper."

"I'll be fine." He regarded her solemnly then cradled her face, his large hand warming her, his thumb stroking her cheek. "Have a good evening."

Burning for him, she eased closer, needing his kiss and caress.

He stepped back then faced a man in the distance and raised his hand in welcome.

Restful sleep wasn't something Nic managed, the slightest noise jerking her awake. Seven o'clock seemed determined not to arrive. At six, she gave up on slumber, showered and dressed then joined her mom and Kanti in the kitchen, breakfast well under way.

Kanti tapped her spatula against the skillet. "Will Ghost be joining us this morning?"

Nic shook her head. "I stocked the guest-house fridge so he'd have something to eat whenever he wanted." Admittedly, a stupid move. If she hadn't provided food, he'd be here, dining with them, making her palms sweaty and her heart yearn. "He'll be by at seven."

"I'll make extra in case he's still hungry." Kanti broke more eggs.

Nic couldn't keep still. By all rights, she should be tending her chores, not having Trent or the ranch hands pick up her slack so she could wait for a man. Only a day had passed since she'd met Ghost and already she required his presence, scent, heat, and smile. After a week, she'd be a basket case.

"You like him, don't you?"

She flinched at her mom's question. "What?"

"I don't blame you." She gave Nic a knowing look. "He's so nice."

"And good-looking." Kanti sighed wistfully. "What a hunk."

Nic laughed. "Shame on you for talking like that. Or even thinking it."

"I'm old, not dead." She turned the eggs. "If you like him, I say go for it. At your age, you shouldn't be alone."

But would be again after he left, the only possible outcome in their work relationship. "He's nice and…good-looking…but he's not here to make me happy."

"No?" Her mom arched one eyebrow. "Then why are you smiling?"

Nic touched her mouth, surprised at her ear-to-ear grin. "I'm not." She killed her glee.

"Whatever you say. Who are the sandwiches for?" Her mom gestured to the pile Nic already made, half beef, half ham. Each for Ghost so they could spend the entire day together without having to return for lunch or dinner or…

You're losing it.

Funny thing, she couldn't stop, didn't want to. "Ghost asked me to show him the ranch. I thought I'd bring food in case we're out long."

Her mom set plates on the table. "Didn't he and his team check out the property last night?"

They had, but she couldn't bring up painful memories by saying he wanted to see where Bryce had died. "They focused on areas where the cattle were or will be. I'm going to show him everything else…just to be extra careful."

No one challenged her lie.

Eating wasn't something she could do, her stomach too unsettled, excitement and desire pumping through her.

At seven sharp, footfalls sounded on the front porch, followed by one hard rap on the door.

"That's him. See you guys later." Nic grabbed her backpack and raced to the front room.

Ghost faced the yard, his rifle hung over one shoulder.

Pulse beating wildly, she stepped outside.

He looked over at her and smiled.

Her knees wilted. He'd shaved and also shampooed his hair, the black strands gleaming in the morning light, his clean skin smelling good enough to lick. It took enormous will for her to keep from jumping him as she wanted. "Morning."

"Hey." He touched her backpack. "What's in here?"

"Snacks." And other stuff she wasn't about to mention now. Hopefully, the appropriate time would present itself later. "Did you have breakfast? Even if you did, Kanti made this for you." Nic pulled two bacon-and-egg sandwiches from her backpack. "Better eat these."

"Gladly. I only had coffee."

"Here." She tugged him to the porch swing. "Sit."

"Nope." He bit into the first sandwich, moaned in delight, then chewed fast and swallowed. "I'd rather get a start on the day. Can you show me the—"

"Yeah. Come on." She hustled him off the porch and kept her voice low. "Don't mention Bryce or his accident anywhere near Kanti or my mom. I don't want them upset."

"Agreed. Sorry. I wasn't thinking."

"Kanti's breakfast sandwiches do that to a man."

He smiled.

Egg dotted his lower lip.

Nic wiped the morsels off then licked them from her finger.

His cheeks darkened.

Her face felt as hot as his looked.

Two ranch hands strolled near, dipped their heads to her and Ghost, then kept glancing at them over their shoulders.

Time to get a grip before everyone on the ranch gossiped about her and the "new" man.

Once they'd reached the garage, Ghost was working on his second sandwich and finished it in three bites. He pointed at a cycle to the rear. "That it?"

"Yeah." Her heart cramped at Bryce's favorite ride. A custom Harley he'd loved, the sleek back resembling a bird's folded wings, the design straight from a sci-fi movie he'd been in. Despite the bent front wheel rim and fender, the vehicle was still in excellent condition. She'd taken care to keep it exactly as it had been on the day he died, in case someone in law enforcement eventually believed her suspicions.

Ghost shoved the empty sandwich wrappers in his pocket then hunkered near the front wheel. "Can you turn on the overhead light?"

She did as he asked. "Would you like the lantern, too?"

"Please." He pointed at an area below the headlamp. "Shine it here."

Once she had, he leaned closer, studying the spot then pulled out his smartphone.

Puzzled, she crouched next to him. "What is it?"

"See this indentation?" He gestured to a spot where the paint had rubbed off. "Notice how thin it is?"

Now that he mentioned it... "From a rock scraping it when it fell over?"

"The depression's too perfect." He took more pictures from different angles.

She pushed to her feet as he did. "What are you thinking?"

"That you're right. Bryce's death wasn't accidental." He scrolled through his photos. "The evidence doesn't add up."

"In what way?"

"Show me the area where he went down, then I'll tell you."

She crossed her arms. "Why not now?"

Ghost inclined his head to the outside. Ranch hands walked past, each peering in the garage before glancing away.

He didn't want an audience, and she couldn't

blame him. "Do you ride?" She gestured to Bryce's many cycles. "It's the best way to see the land."

"A horse is better...given what's already happened." His gaze slid to the ruined cycle.

Nic wasn't sure what he was getting at and figured he wouldn't tell her until they were away from the garage and house. "I'll have one of the hands saddle up two horses for us."

"One's good enough." Sin registered in his eyes, desire tightening his features.

Her heart skipped several beats then pounded, hurting her chest. "Okay."

CHAPTER 4

Nic rode in front on the gelding, Ghost behind, her backpack and his rifle secured to the saddle.

With impressive skill, he guided their horse past the living quarters to open land, the crew and her family left behind, the day breathtaking —sun bright, sky clear, flowers and grass scenting the soft breeze.

He eased his arm around her waist.

Her pulse jumped, heat pouring through her. Unable to resist, she released her weight into him. Her lids grew heavy at his size and strength, his rigid cock nestled against her ass.

Holding her tightly yet gently, too, he leaned over her shoulder. "Which way?"

She hadn't a clue what he meant, their lips mere inches away...kissing territory. "For what?"

"Where Bryce went down."

Right. The true purpose for their ride. That reality didn't crush her desire, the feelings too intense and welcomed. Finding her voice proved difficult, but she managed. "To the south, past the third stand of trees on the right."

He straightened and kept the horse at a gentle pace.

She hoped because he wanted to enjoy this time with her, but good sense said there could be another explanation. "Are you going so slowly because you're afraid we might encounter what Bryce did when he fell from the bike?"

"I can't be sure. Until I am, it's wise to be careful."

The reason he hadn't wanted her to ride alone and risk injury. Disappointment gripped her even though it shouldn't have. He was at the ranch for protection not romance. Getting her bearings, she settled down to business, surprised at how he avoided the trees even when they were widely separated and easy to traverse, no low-hanging branches or protruding rocks to worry about. Paths Bryce liked best, weaving his cycle between barriers as he'd frequently done in his films.

She turned her face to the side, catching Ghost's scent, musk tinging the light fragrance. Her head spun. "Uh…" Her thoughts grew so muddled she couldn't voice more.

He pressed closer. "What?"

Don't ever move. Stay like this forever. A dumb hope she couldn't abide and shook off her arousal. "Do you think Victor and his men have watched Bryce's films?"

"Not anywhere they'd have to pay. That would leave a paper trail. Of course, a computer records history, even when someone thinks they've deleted it. So if they saw his films on YouTube…"

She gripped the saddle horn. "You're saying they knew he liked to weave between trees?"

"It's the only thing that makes sense since Bryce was a seasoned rider and knew his land well. He didn't take foolish risks." Ghost reined in the gelding close to a nearby stand. "Is this the spot?"

"Over there." She pointed.

He dismounted first and helped her down then strode to where she'd found Bryce.

Awful memories bombarded her—his prone figure, how his head lay at an unnatural angle, her screaming then shouting for him to wake up, shaking him to make him do so, finally accepting the horrible truth and sobbing. She wrapped her arms around herself.

Ghost touched her shoulder. "You okay?"

"Yeah. Let's do this."

He looked like he wanted to say more but, instead, circled the area where Bryce had been then eyed the trees and squatted near the first. When he ran his hand over the trunk then took pictures on his smartphone, she joined him. "What is it?"

"The same thin line we saw on the bike."

She bent over, surprised at the groove in the wood. "What made that?"

"Wire." Stooped by the opposite tree, he pressed his thumbnail into a similar groove then snapped more shots and straightened. "It's possible Victor's men strung a line from this tree to that one. Once they did, it was a simple matter to wait. When Bryce hit the booby-trap at fifty miles an hour or so, the cycle stopped, he didn't. My guess is he flew over the handlebars and landed on his head."

As the actor Christopher Reeve had done while riding his horse, which caused his quadriplegia. In his case, there were witnesses to the accident, affording him immediate medical attention and a chance to live. Not so for Bryce. He'd died out here alone, unable to call for help or breathe, slowly suffocating. A sob caught in her throat.

"Nic..." Ghost gathered her to him and rubbed her back. "I shouldn't have asked you to take me here. Trent could have done so. I'm sorry. I didn't mean to add to your grief."

"You haven't. If anything, you've given me hope." She gripped his T-shirt, her face pressed to his neck. "I want Victor to pay for what he's done."

"He will, I swear." He tightened his hold, his heart thumping as hard as hers. "I won't stop until he does."

"I know. I..." Too much loneliness and yearning kept her from holding back. She kissed his neck, jaw, cheek, lips, her lust insatiable.

A pleased growl rushed from him. He pulled her close and fitted his mouth to hers.

Weakened and yielding, she suckled his tongue slavishly, drawing it deeper inside, loving his clean taste. Longing for more, she pulled him closer and wrapped her leg around his.

A primitive noise erupted from him. He cupped her ass and pulled her into his erection, his cock thick as hell, harder than stone.

They struggled to get nearer, each demanding full satisfaction, holding nothing back.

At last, her lungs burned, needing a full breath.

He broke free first and gulped air.

Wind whipped around them. Birds cried out overhead.

Panting, she cradled his face. "Take me to the guesthouse." She kissed him again, harder this time, more desperately, too.

He matched her frenzy, clutching at her clothes as she did his, cupping his balls and dick as he squeezed her breast.

Still fondling each other, they lurched to the gelding.

On the ride back, Ghost urged their horse to a gallop.

At the guesthouse, he tethered the animal while she untied his rifle and her backpack, then delivered the firearm to him.

He heaved air as hard as she did, their breaths

shallow and halting. After hanging the weapon on his shoulder, he lifted her into his arms, and kissed her deeply.

His lips were softer than a flower petal, this moment a miracle she'd waited for too long. Melted against him, she pushed his tongue from her mouth and filled his instead, unable to deny herself.

As their tongues dueled and their kiss grew savage, he edged toward the porch and blindly climbed the stairs, his steps small and cautious, giving their passion additional time.

She wasn't about to complain.

Hinges squeaked.

He'd opened the front door. How, she didn't know or care. Using his shoulder, he pushed it in, bypassed the brief kitchen and dining area then lowered her to her feet by the double bed.

Too quickly, she missed his mouth, taste, warmth, and size.

The moment he shut and locked the door, she dropped her knapsack, gripped his T-shirt, and yanked him to the bed.

Together, they dropped to the mattress.

The frame groaned, springs popped.

Boots and clothes flew.

Naked, they clung to each other, their kisses fevered, noisy and wet.

Rough sounds spilled from him. He rolled them from side to side, at last settling her on top, her pussy against his cock, boobs crushed against his chest. As one they lingered, lust quieted, their passion tender and exploring.

Her heart opened more to him than it should but she couldn't stave off her emotions. She wanted him to love her, needed him at her side for as long as he could stay.

The future wasn't something she wanted to consider now. She had a lifetime to live without him.

Stop it. Enjoy what you have.

She gentled her desire further, savoring the man he was, allowing him what he willed.

He squeezed her breast carefully as though fearing he'd hurt her but then thumbed and plucked her nipple like the bad boy he was.

Nerve endings fired, tingling her skin. Breathing wasn't easy, but she panted as well as she could around his tongue and fondled his balls.

He made a noise more animal than human and tore his mouth from hers. "Do that again and

I'm a goner. Then the party's over before it's begun."

"Got it. Hang tight." She crawled across the mattress.

"Whoa." He grabbed her ankle. "Where do you think you're going?"

"Backpack." She pointed. "To get the rubbers."

"No need. They're here, too." He leaned over and pulled a string from the top nightstand drawer.

Odd. When she'd cleaned here yesterday, there hadn't been any inside. "Yours?"

A sheepish look crossed his face. "Bought them yesterday evening in town while you were in the main house. I thought…I hoped…"

"Damn right you should have. If you hadn't, there would have been hell to pay."

Laughing, he fell back.

His position gave her the perfect opportunity to straddle his thighs and enjoy his masculine bounty.

His skin was a solid copper tint, no tan lines marring the perfection, his chest broad and smooth, pecs and abs superbly defined, chestnut nipples small, stomach hard and flat.

Excitement coiled and built within her, heat stinging her face and throat.

She cradled his long, thick cock, its root nested in thick black curls, passion darkening the ruddy head, pre-cum glistening on the tiny slit. His balls were as beautiful—plump and tight, dark hairs lightly furring them, masculine as fuck. Never had she been as hungry for a man's flesh and scooted down to taste him.

"Uh-uh." He hauled her back up and held her in his firm grip. "I want inside your sweet cunt. Now."

Who was she to argue? Intense longing blazed in his eyes, proving she wasn't a simple lay to him. She meant something. He liked and respected her as a person.

She'd never meet another man like him.

Despite his quickened breaths, she took her time sheathing his cock, needing to draw out the anticipation and pleasure.

He sucked in more air. "Want me to help so we can get a move on?"

Once they did, these moments would be over, never to return. Unable to voice her thoughts, she shook her head.

"Hey." He eased her hair behind her ears and cupped her chin. "What's wrong?"

Lying was easier than the truth. "Got a cramp in my foot. It's gone now."

"Sure? Want me to massage it?"

"No." She drank him in, burning his tousled hair, searching gaze, and sincere concern into her brain, the memory tucked safely away for another day when she'd need something good to sustain her. "Make love to me."

Pleasure lit his features. Using more grace than earlier, he rolled them over, until she lay beneath him, and then brushed his mouth against hers.

Their breaths collided.

Bodies touched.

The world paused, leaving nothing except him and her.

His newest kiss proved more wondrous than the others, uninhibited yet sweet, touching every chord. Without breaking stride, he entered her on one powerful thrust, burrowing his cock deep into her sheath, their curls touching.

She soared, loving his weight and heat, his musk enthralling her and increasing her dizziness, the room seeming to twirl around them.

New moisture streamed from her already drenched pussy, proving her rapture, welcoming him farther inside.

Accepting the unspoken invitation, he drove deeper.

She gripped his shoulders, wanting him to become one with her blood and soul, not caring if she lost restraint. From little on, she'd learned to be brave. For once, she needed to live.

He pumped slowly, an easy slide in and out of her. An enchanting act she never wanted him to stop, hungering for this to last throughout the day and well into tomorrow morning when they'd rest. Though only to regain strength and begin anew.

His pace quickened slightly. He thumbed her clit.

Delight shot through her, her ears buzzing. She bucked and gasped around his tongue.

He pushed it deeper into her mouth, quieting her. Taking what he willed, what she'd eagerly allowed him, coordinating his thrusts and strokes for maximum pleasure.

A familiar ache filled her pussy, seeking relief, her climax already edging too close too quickly.

No. She tensed, fighting her approaching

orgasm, her shoulders burning, neck aching, her pussy not giving a damn about her pain, wanting nothing except its due. Her sheath grew narrower or his cock had thickened. No matter, the friction between them increased, pushing her nearer the edge.

Resisting, she gripped the sheets.

He thumbed her nub harder, faster, timing his finger-fuck to his unrestrained thrusts.

The bed shook, springs squeaked.

Their harsh breathing added to the fray.

The surroundings whirled, not letting her catch up. Perspiration ran down her temples and neck. Her pussy screamed for release.

It crashed into her, flinging her past constraint to a place where she spun and floated, panted and fought for breath, trembled from euphoria then drooped, too exhausted to budge, except for her wildly pulsing pussy.

Crazy fucking good.

But not enough. Ghost hadn't had his fun.

Nic forced her lids to part.

Teeth clenched, he pumped as if his life depended upon it, his complexion darkened to a dangerous point, sweat dotting his upper lip, hair swaying.

She cupped his face. "Come. Please."

"Not yet."

"When?"

"In a—" He stiffened, his eyes bulging, and then he howled.

A magnificent sound, his male beast freed.

After several additional thrusts, he shuddered, sank to his elbows, and rested his forehead on her chest. "Wow."

She giggled. "I'll say. Want to go again?"

"Uh…" He trembled and blew out a breath. "In a bit."

"Would you like to sleep?"

"No." He fought for air.

"Sure?"

"Ah…okay, maybe a little." After he shook off a yawn, it returned and consumed him. He swore beneath his breath. "If you don't mind."

He sounded so apologetic, her heart opened even more to him. "Never."

If she'd been a bolder person, she would have confessed how much she liked him already and that he was the first man she might be able to love. *Yeah, sure.* Better not hit him with such a heavy burden, especially when he was too weary to bolt.

She smoothed his hair. "Relax."

He promptly tongued her nipple into his mouth and sucked.

Typical man, yet also marvelously unique, making her toes curl and turning her brain to mush.

His suckling slowed then stopped, his breathing growing deeper, sleep descending upon him.

Relaxed and sated for the moment, she soon followed.

CHAPTER 5

WHEN GHOST WAS seven years old, his maternal grandfather introduced him to a world few in this country would experience firsthand. The wealth, alone, proved unimaginable even by Hollywood standards. A life where a whim for anything and everything was never too much to grant. To most, a veritable Xanadu.

He couldn't escape quickly enough.

To him, nothing matched the homey comfort Nic's guesthouse provided. Watching her sleep was a gift he treasured.

She lay curled on her side, dark hair grazing her cheek, lips parted on quiet breaths, one hand held to her heart, the other outstretched to him, her mind and body achieving peace at last. He suspected she hadn't slept this well since Bryce's murder.

Lightheaded and longing, he never wanted to leave her side, everything he was and would be kneeling to her. He'd never known a braver or more exquisite woman. Her creamy skin called to the male within him, stiffening his cock. Her strawberry-colored nipples were delightfully tight, the tips erect.

Moisture glistened on her dark bush, remnants from their lovemaking. With her, he could never abide an emotionless fuck. From the moment she'd pointed her rifle at him, threatening to shoot off his balls, she'd owned his heart.

His smile felt good...comfortable...because he'd found home.

God knew, he'd searched long enough.

She stirred, splaying then curling her toes, stretching her long legs, pushing her hair back.

He liked her newest earrings, long jobs, the feathers turquoise, brown, and white. The jewelry her only embellishment. She wore no makeup, not even lipstick, and didn't need any. No cosmetic could improve on nature.

Her lids fluttered.

That's it, baby, wake up. I don't want to be alone.

She opened one eye, glanced at his grin, then offered her own. "You're awake."

Hard, too. "Yep. For hours."

Her gaze shot to the windows. The sun had barely budged. They'd been out maybe twenty minutes or so. "You're a terrible liar."

"I know." Elbow on the mattress, he propped his head in his hand and fingered her earring. "I learned as much when I was a kid. No matter what shit rained down, lies never saved my ass. Eventually, I gave up and spoke the truth, no matter how much it hurt me."

Worry crossed her face. "Your folks were hard on you?"

"Never." Even after so many years, boundless love welled in him, softening his voice. "My dad was the kindest soul you'd ever know. Never had a bad word for anyone. Mom was even gentler. Not once did she lose her temper. She listened rather than interrupted, explained instead of demanded. They were the best people ever."

Nic pushed to a sitting position and rested her hand on his. "Were?"

Grief tightened his throat. He cleared it. "When

I was six, they died in a car accident a few miles from the reservation. A teenage driver plowed into their pickup. From what the reports said, the kid and his girlfriend had been necking while he barreled down the road. They thought it was a cool thing to do and walked away without a scratch."

Her face went white. "Oh my God, I'm so sorry." She hugged him fiercely then touched the scar on his cheek. "I'd guessed this was from your time in the service, but you got it in the accident?"

"I wasn't with them. My aunt was babysitting me until they returned from their date night. My grandparents were already gone by then, leaving only Dad and his older sister. I didn't get the scar until I was twelve."

She stroked the uneven skin. "Did you fall off a horse or your skateboard?"

The past rose to torment him, as it had too many times, populating his solitary moments and nightmares. "I refused to go to a party my maternal grandfather insisted I attend. Not because he was proud of who I was. He said my kind needed civilizing. I didn't agree. He beat me with his belt. The buckle slashed my cheek."

"Lord." She clutched her throat. "Was he insane?"

"Mean. He never forgave my mother, his daughter, for taking up with my dad, a lousy Indian from the reservation. They met through mutual friends. Money didn't mean anything to her or to him. They simply wanted to love each other and build a life, have a family. Mom was three months pregnant when she died. Grandfather had her buried in the family plot in The Hamptons despite how my aunt protested. Didn't matter. He couldn't separate my parents during life, but he sure as fuck could do so after death. Then he fought to adopt me, the little savage. That's what he called me around the help and his acquaintances."

Her chin trembled. "If he hated your dad, why would he want you?"

"Power. To prove no one got the better of him. He always won. Not because he wanted something, but because he achieved it no matter the odds, while destroying his opponent in the process."

She scooted closer and held his face. "How long did the beatings go on?"

At the time, the abuse seemed like forever.

Even in retrospect, he wasn't certain how he'd survived. "Until I was thirteen. By then, I was taller and stronger. When he lit into me that last day, I grabbed his arm and promised if he ever laid a hand on me again, I'd kill him, but before I did, I'd make damn certain he'd know what a real savage I was. For the first time, true fear filled his eyes."

The man's aged face rose in Ghost's thoughts, his pasty skin ashen from panic, eyes goggled in horror. "I'm not sorry." Turning the other cheek wasn't possible around people like his grandfather. They respected nothing except power. "I never will be. After that, he left me alone, spending most of his time in Europe. I wanted to run away but was wise enough to know I'd never make it on the street. My aunt had passed the previous year, and I wasn't sure if my people would take me back on the reservation, considering how Grandfather had hounded them with lawsuits concerning his claim to me. Trent's family offered a home, but they were having a hard time as it was. I couldn't become their next burden. With nowhere else to go, I stayed in Grandfather's mansion until I was seventeen then joined the

Army. By then, I wanted to be continents away from him and his kind. If I hadn't been, I might have acted out again. God knows what I would have done."

"Nothing." She stroked his hair. "You're not a violent man by nature."

"I can be. I proved it then."

"He pushed you to a breaking point. You were a lonely kid defending yourself. I know it's politically correct and spiritual to forgive someone who's killed a family member or made your life hell. I call BS on that." Loathing filled her eyes. "How can you absolve anyone who would do it again if they had a chance? Monsters like that deserve to die."

Given her background, her fury didn't surprise him. He gathered her close. "Once you and your mom escaped your father, did he come to the ranch and try to harm you again?"

She lowered her face and shook her head. "I don't think he ever knew we were here. We were originally from Nevada. The last I heard, he died in prison during a fight."

Ghost couldn't have asked for a better resolution. "What was he doing time for?"

She shivered. "Beating his newborn then

strangling his girlfriend when she tried to intervene."

Jesus. "Was the child okay?"

"Newspaper reports said the boy never regained consciousness, so they took him off life support. My father fled, but the law caught up with him in Vegas. He was trying to reestablish connections there to help him escape to Mexico. He had another girlfriend in Tijuana. She came to the States to attend his trial, cheering him on, saying the mother had actually hurt the child and he became so enraged he strangled her in retaliation. Reporters played up the angle to create doubt and interest, saying he could be innocent. I called the District Attorney, reporting what he put my mom and me through and offered to testify against him. Because I was so young when he brutalized Mom, they wanted her testimony instead. She was too afraid. I don't blame her. I shouldn't have interfered."

"You did what you thought was right. The only thing that matters is they put him away and he's gone."

She lifted her face to his. "What about your grandfather?"

"He passed five years ago. His lawyer

contacted me to say he'd written me out of his will. Since he'd already disinherited my mother when she hooked up with my dad, I wouldn't get a dime. I thanked the woman. She told me I shouldn't be resentful. I explained I wasn't. I'd never been more relieved in my life. Now Satan could deal with him." He grinned at the memory. "She inhaled sharply at my comment. Offended, I'm sure, by my honesty. Like you said, and I agreed, I'm a lousy liar."

"You have other talents." She touched his still sheathed cock.

The damn thing shot to attention, blossoming within her touch, not wanting bad memories any longer, only a bright future. "You want to talk some more?"

"I've had enough of the past. How about you?" She cradled his balls.

Pleasure shot everywhere, his breath snagging. *Nice.* But for now, he wanted to run this show. After ditching the rubber, he pushed her to the mattress.

"Hey." She blew hair off her face and struggled to her elbows. "I want to eat you. Lie down."

"Later." Positioned between her thighs, he propped her calves on his shoulders, spreading her wide, exposing her puffy folds, her arousal dampening them. He inhaled deeply, pulling in her musk. *God.* Nothing on earth matched her fragrance. His balls twitched, and his cock hardened enough to sting, needing her cunt. *In time. First this.* He pressed his face to her springy curls.

A wanting sigh poured from her.

If he could have vocalized his delight, he would have, but too much need filled him to allow a full breath, her delicate scent driving him wild, making him impatient.

He held her clit between his teeth and licked the rigid nub.

She gasped.

Love sounds he adored and couldn't live without any longer. His entire life had been an endless journey to reach her side, the only woman he wanted. Now that he was here, he had to give her his best and deliver whatever pleasure he could.

He kept his licks slow yet steady as he slipped two fingers into her cunt while also probing her anus.

She cried out but pressed closer, telling him she wanted more.

After teasing her clit, he retreated to keep her

from coming too quickly. He worked his fingers in and out of her pussy, as he would his cock, and eased his pinkie into her tightest opening.

She beat the mattress and squirmed, though not enough to break his hold on her. Her oaths flew next, some in English, then Spanish, followed by her praising him in Blackfoot.

Incalculable emotion rose, constricting his throat. Nothing could have touched him more than her knowing his native language, another bond between them.

Even so, sentiment didn't encourage him to let her climax.

Each time she drew close, he abandoned her nub until she calmed. The second she did, he resumed his torment.

Grunts and groans escaped her, followed by Blackfoot commands for him to get on with it.

Not a chance.

She gripped the sheet and growled. "Let. Me. Fucking. Come!"

When he was good and ready. Until then...

Doubling down, he worked her clit, cunt, and anus.

She blubbered something he didn't understand then swore again in English. Perspiration drenched her torso, throat, and face, her chest pumping hard on each torturous breath.

She'd never been more inviting to him.

"Please." She ground her fists into her eyes. "I can't stand one more—"

He picked up his pace, going at her nub and cunt without pause.

Her shout filled the room, gasps replacing it, her pussy contracting around his fingers, each pulse hard and telling, verifying her orgasm.

Pleased at her delight and smug at his prowess, he lowered her legs to the mattress and offered his best smile. "You're welcome."

She opened one eye and gave him the finger.

Laughing, he rested his chin on her bush. "It was my pleasure."

"Oh, please." She pushed to her elbows and gulped air. "You nearly killed me. I had no idea you could be such a prick."

"No?" He straightened, his cock defying gravity on its own and pointing at her. "Do you need glasses?"

She worked her mouth to hide her smile. "After I get through with you, you might go blind."

Before he could respond, she shoved him back.

Losing his balance, he hit the mattress, shaking it.

She cupped his balls firmly, not enough to hurt but to insure his compliance. "Try to stop me and you'll find out what I'm really made of."

"I already did when you wanted to shoot off my nuts."

"I was playing then." She shrugged. "Not now." She eased his right ball into her mouth.

Holy fuck. His hair stood on end, her wet heat warmer than the fucking sun. Too much pleasure roared through him, touching each part before zooming back to his groin and intensifying.

His cock felt as if it were two feet long and weighed a ton. "I can't— You have to— Fuck, I'm going to—"

No matter how hard he tried, he couldn't form a complete sentence to beg her to stop, to give him a moment so he wouldn't come. He pummeled the mattress.

While it quivered, she alternately suckled and licked his ball and masturbated his cock better than he'd ever done.

Shit, shit, shit. "Give me a sec!"

She tongued his nut from her mouth. "Hush."

He panted. "What?"

In answer, she took his other ball between her lips.

Argh. Don't come, don't come, don't—

Helpless against her, he had nothing except raw determination to keep from blowing his wad.

Sweat poured down his face. His cock hurt like a son of a bitch, wanting relief he refused to give. His balls felt close to bursting.

Desperate to distract himself, he relived the worst times in his life: his parents' death, leaving the reservation, his first night in the mansion, not knowing how to react to his grandfather's racial slurs and contempt, wanting to run away, not knowing where to go, wondering if he'd ever have a real home again, meeting Nic, liking her from the start, admiring her courage and character, needing her more than he had anyone else...

Stop!

He couldn't, too focused on her.

Thankfully, she halted and released his ball.

Unknotting his shoulders and neck proved impossible, but at least he could breathe again.

She licked his inner thigh.

He writhed at the tickling, laughter spilling from him.

Pressed close, she took his cock into her mouth clear to her tonsils, her nose touching his hairy groin.

"*Fuck.*"

"Mmm." She made noises like a woman gorging on chocolate rather than his sex, her sucking wicked, licks intense. Each time she trapped his crown between her lips, she lapped the bumpy skin in back, his most sensitive spot.

He splayed his toes so much, his left foot cramped. The pain did shit to ease his excitement or need. This much delight couldn't be sound. If he didn't come soon, his dick would fucking fall off.

Interminably, she drove his cock in and out of her mouth, adding a twist and rapid licks to torment him further.

He tugged the sheet. The linen pulled away from the mattress.

Unmindful, she fondled his balls, her thumbnail scraping lightly over their contours.

Every-fucking-thing on him tingled, even his gums. Taking a breath wasn't possible any longer. Imploring her to slow the hell down weren't words he could form.

She'd taken his will and strength, pleasure replacing them.

His climax exploded, his cum filling her mouth.

Ringing sounded in his ears, drowning out everything else, his throat and chest aching from his heart slamming into them. Lifting his hand was an effort he couldn't accomplish. His legs were watery, thighs twitching, balls compressing as they emptied their load.

Nic didn't back away from his ejaculate. After drinking it, she licked the last traces off his cock and balls.

Holy fucking Christ. Her tongue sent his pulse racing, the feelings she produced too intense.

Using what little energy he had, he gripped her wrist. "Stop. Please. I can't stand more."

She lifted her chin. "You're welcome."

He laughed wearily.

Carrie Underwood's "Before He Cheats" played.

Surprised, he pushed up slightly. The sound came from in here rather than outside. Had to be

Nic's ringtone. His played Tim McGraw's "Live Like You Were Dying."

She groaned. "I better get that. Could be my mom or Kanti." She rolled across the bed, pulled her phone from the backpack, and looked at the screen. "It's Mom." She brought the phone to her ear. "Hey." While listening, she glanced at Ghost's cock, her moisture still dampening it. "Yeah, we're getting a lot done."

He rubbed his mouth to keep from laughing.

She gave him a look then frowned and spoke to her mother. "Wait. What did you say?" After listening, she shook her head. "As far as we can tell, Victor's men haven't been on other parts of the ranch." She shot Ghost a guilty look, but her voice was steady, her lies believable. "If we do, we'll let you know."

He figured she'd tell her mom and Kanti the bare minimum, and only to keep them safe.

She listened then straightened, panic in her eyes. "Where are we now?" She looked at him for help.

He came up empty on what to tell her, but finally pointed at the door.

She mouthed, "What?"

He flung out his arm to indicate she should tell her mom they were far away from here.

Frustration deepened her frown. She gripped the phone. "Uh…we just reached the east forty. Why?" She listened then closed her eyes. "Right. I shouldn't have forgotten. I'll get on it immediately. Talk to you later. Bye." She ended the call and drooped. "Hell."

"What's wrong?" Besides his lousy assistance.

"I need to make a run into town for groceries. Kanti's out of flour and bacon and…hell." Nic curled her fingers around his ankle. "I'm sorry."

"No need. I'll go with you."

"Uh-uh." She dropped her phone into the backpack. "You should stay here and rest up for later."

Sounded promising. "I can do that on the way to town and back. You drive, I'll sleep."

She ran her thumb over his anklebone. "You're sure?"

"I don't lie well. Remember?"

Beaming, she hugged him. "Thanks. By the way, she wanted to know what we've found out. Guess you heard me saying that, huh? Please don't tell her about the Bryce thing."

"It's your call and your right to let her know. However, I did do other things."

"Such as? Wait. When?"

"While you were sleeping."

She sat cross-legged on the mattress, her delicate folds displayed to him, their deep-pink color matching her nipples. "What did you do?"

"Sent the pictures of Bryce's motorcycle and those trees to law enforcement I know in another county. They're good guys. Contacted a lab about getting the cigarette butts DNA tested and arranged for a vet in a neighboring county to necropsy the cows."

She gaped then cringed. "I can't pay for that."

"I'm taking care of it."

"No, you're not." She squeezed his toes enough to hurt. "I can't let you."

"It's already done and paid for, so please don't rip off my foot."

Shock crossed her face. She looked down and released him. "Sorry. But you still shouldn't do this."

"I want to. Let me be a hero."

Corny words, but they had the desired effect. She softened, wonder filling her gaze. "You're far more than that."

"Yeah? I expect you to fill in the details later. Right now, we should go."

"Damn straight. The faster we finish, the sooner we can come back here for the important stuff."

Sounded like the best plan ever to him.

CHAPTER 6

Nic took Bryce's pickup, Ghost riding shotgun, his weapon literally at his side.

She wasn't certain why he'd insisted on taking the rifle, but she didn't ask and wasn't about to argue.

In the supermarket, they shopped like an old married couple—rather than the new lovers they were—comparing labels, debating price and quality, warning each other about too rich food and cholesterol.

Okay, she did that, but her sage advice didn't convince him to put back the fried pork rinds or toaster pastries. "Those strudel things are nothing but fat, sugar, and salt, held together by chemicals."

He cradled the box to his chest. "When I lived with my grandfather, the cook snuck me these when I was sad, which was pretty much all the time. They bring back good memories."

Plus rotting his teeth and clogging his arteries. "For real?"

"Naw." He grinned. "My grandfather's cook made the witch in the *Wizard of Oz* look like Mother Teresa. I stole junk food from the kids at the school Grandfather insisted I attend, uniforms and all. Those trust-fund brats had enough bucks on them to entice local markets to deliver whatever they ordered to the academy. When I was hungry, I got crap like carrot sticks and apple slices from the cafeteria."

It seemed his grandfather wanted him healthy and alive to prolong his suffering. She certainly didn't want to give him more grief. "At least you don't smoke."

He put the items in their cart. "Did I say anything about the chocolate-filled donut you wanted at the bakery counter then gobbled without taking a breath the moment I paid for it, or the M&Ms currently lying on the bacon?"

She'd tossed two extra-large bags in with their other stuff.

Busted, she stroked his cheek. "You're a good man. Wise, too."

"Because you'd knee me in the balls if I'd said a word?"

She laughed.

An elderly patron approached, her hair and skin whiter than sun-bleached bones. She scowled at them.

Ghost tipped his head in greeting and offered a sweet smile.

She sniffed and hurried away.

Turd. Not that Nic could voice her opinion. People of color were rare in this supermarket and town. Living here was a throwback to the South during pre-civil rights days when no one saw the darkies unless they entered their segregated territories.

Martin Luther King must be spinning in his grave. He couldn't have imagined the hatred would have festered this long, flaring up stronger and hotter these past years.

At least she wasn't alone today, Ghost's presence offering safety and comfort.

She took his hand. He squeezed hers.

Once they'd filled their cart, checked out, and loaded the truck, she raced to the ranch.

"Better slow down." He didn't look up from his smartphone. "Deputies might be around. My guess is they'll want to give you more than a speeding ticket."

Like a bullet to the head? Not wanting to bring up unpleasant shit, she didn't share her thoughts. "My bad." She slowed to a reasonable speed.

He rested his hand on her thigh and scrolled through something on his screen.

"What's so interesting?"

"Got a few text messages from the team about their patrol and where they'll be tonight."

She placed his palm on her pussy. "I know where you'll be."

"For hours and hours." He leaned across the console and pecked her cheek, his stubble rasping her skin, his breath heating it. "Maybe you should hit the gas."

Grinning, she did, then slammed on the brakes.

The pickup rocked.

"Shit." He gripped the seat. "Are you okay?"

No.

"Nic, answer me!" He touched her leg, arm, shoulder. "What happened?"

Rather than look at him, she faced the windshield—what waited for them in the distance. "We have visitors."

Several men from Victor's crew stood shoulder to shoulder blocking the entrance to her ranch. The pricks had even set up sawhorses. All were armed.

Ghost grabbed his rifle. "Stay here."

"No." She clutched his wrist. "I'll handle this."

"What? They're armed."

"So am I." She pulled out her smartphone. Before Ghost could respond, she left the pickup and approached the group, phone raised and recording. "Get off my land!"

The brawny man in front stepped forward, greasy hair clinging to his scalp, naked chest and belly protruding from his leather vest, his gang's name and colors on the upper right, too far away for her to read. "Ain't your land. Never has been. This portion belongs to Mr. Victor. He's claiming it. We're here to see you don't trespass no more."

Shocked, she couldn't find words.

The men behind him chuckled. Some wore caps displaying their supremacist roots. Each bore garish tattoos and ugly smiles.

She should have been afraid but outrage

seethed within her, making her oddly calm. "He has no right to this property. Never did. Court after court has ruled against him."

"He doesn't listen to a government that has no authority over him. The only rightful law in these parts is the sheriff, and he agrees with Mr. Victor and us. Now run along before you force us to get physical with you."

Her skin crawled at the thought of him or the others touching her, but only death would make her retreat. "We'll see what the highway patrol says when they get here."

"This is a private road, bitch. Mr. Victor's private road."

"Not the one my pickup is on." She lowered the phone to call the authorities even if they weren't the proper ones. She had to get someone out here to help.

The man in front glared and spoke to the others. "Take that damn phone away from her then bring her to me. I'll show her who's boss."

Two men broke rank, both smoking cigarettes.

Shots rang out.

Bullets hit the dirt a breath away from their boots.

They reared back.

More shots cracked, as loud as thunder in the still air. One man's cigarette flew from his hand, arced, and dropped to the ground, pulverized by the bullet. The other man's smoke disappeared, or so it seemed. What was left of it lay in the dirt near his feet.

Ghost approached, rifle pointed, finger on the trigger. He shouted, "One move, just one, and my next shots will part your goddamn hair and singe the hair on your nuts before you can blink, then I'll go in for the fucking kill."

He fired again. His shot came so close to the lead man's hand; he must have felt its heat and dropped his rifle.

Ghost stepped forward again, firing at their feet, driving them back, shouting over the noise. "Want to guess how many of you I can take down before you squeeze off one shot?"

The intruders scattered, taking off across the land toward Victor's ranch.

Before they vanished over the gentle hill, Ghost had his phone to his ear and spoke to whomever he'd called. "I want the entire patrol down at the ranch entrance now. Tell Nic's people to station themselves at each entry point leading into the property, everyone armed and ready for trouble. I'll explain further when you get here." He ended the call.

She touched his arm. "Are you all right?"

"Are you?"

"Yeah, they never got close. I filmed them." She held up her phone.

He glanced at it then at an area past her. "Looks like someone dropped his cell."

Sunlight glinted off the device. "I'll get it." She brought it back to him. "At least now we'll know this person's name."

"I'm hoping for a lot more." He slipped the phone into his pocket, hung his rifle over his shoulder, then gripped her arms. "What in the hell is the matter with you approaching those goons by yourself? Did you want them to kill you or rape you first then put a bullet in your head?"

"Of course not." She tried to pull away.

He wouldn't let her.

She slumped. "I was worried about you. I didn't want them ganging up and doing anything because of your heritage."

"If that's the case, you'd have to protect me from most people in this county."

"I will. I intend to." She'd die for him. Not a

silly romantic notion, the right one. They'd gotten Bryce, but couldn't have Ghost. Even if she never saw him again after today, he was hers to protect while here.

He mumbled something beneath his breath.

She guessed it wasn't sweet nothings. "What's the matter? You don't like a woman taking charge?"

A smile tugged at his lips. He killed it and gave her a look. "You did just fine in bed. Out here's different. Although I appreciate your concern, I won't have you risking your safety. I can take care of myself."

"I saw." Nothing in recent memory had dazzled her more. "Damn. You are one fine shot. Smart as fuck, too."

Puzzlement crossed his face. "Meaning?"

"You didn't draw blood or injure those SOBs in any way, giving them reason to have you arrested for attempted murder and to sue me for hiring help I can't control. If that had happened, Victor would have surely bankrupted me with a civil suit and taken everything."

Ghost rubbed his forehead. "I don't kill unless I have to. If they'd laid one finger on you…"

"They didn't. It's over."

Motors sounded, pickups barreling from the ranch toward them, tires stirring up dust. His team.

He looked at her. "Go to the main house, please."

Her stomach fell. "I thought we were going to the guesthouse."

"I have to talk to my men and do other things. I won't be back for a while."

She wanted to argue her point but couldn't bring him more trouble. Reluctantly, she stepped back. "No matter how long you take, I'll wait for you in our bed."

Once in her pickup, she drove past him and around the barriers to deliver the promised groceries.

CHAPTER 7

THROUGHOUT THE AFTERNOON, Nic avoided the main house as much as she could, uncertain if she could hide her worry from her mom and Kanti. She begged off lunch, offering a lame excuse as to checking on the new calves then resuming her and Ghost's perusal across the land. "I don't know when I'll be back. Please don't wait dinner."

The older women looked hopeful, Kanti speaking first. "You and Ghost are getting along?"

Her mother jumped in. "And hitting it off?"

They had no idea. His scent, touch, voice, and laughter took up permanent residence in Nic's thoughts, the same as her worry over whether he was all right.

She haunted the guesthouse porch, dreading every unusual noise that might represent gunfire, her stomach queasy, palms damp. Uneasiness made her too skittish to sit on the swing. Pacing, she considered Victor's men descending upon the ranch en masse, guns drawn and firing, like in a bad Western. Realistically, the scenario seemed unlikely. Bullies didn't take the offense against a stronger opponent. They were too cowardly and proved it when Ghost had run them off. Their next move would be shrewder, as in ambushing him.

Crap. She bit her lip hard enough to draw blood and pulled out her phone but couldn't call him. He was a grown man, a bodyguard, and an ex-military sniper who'd seen worse in his overseas missions than anything Victor's men could dole out here.

He can take care of himself. His kickass shooting proved that. *You need to chill.*

She did her best and retreated inside to review what she'd filmed. The shots were relatively steady, the lead creep framed well, several slimeballs behind him also in focus and, hopefully, recognizable to those who might know them, the audio perfect.

Wanting more details, she chanced a trip to the main house to grab her laptop. To Nic's relief, Kanti and her mom worked in the garden, tending their carrots, potatoes, green beans, and cucumbers.

Back at the guesthouse, she scoured the net for motorcycle gang symbols, locating the one on the jerk's vest. Next, she looked up the acronyms stitched on the caps some wore and recorded the supremacist groups' names.

YouTube offered numerous documentaries, detailing domestic terrorists and outlaw gangs spouting their racist filth. Their attacks on innocent people brought bile to her throat, but also gave her an idea.

While she researched her plans, the front door opened.

Her pulse leaped. She shot to her feet, the kitchen chair wobbling.

Ghost stopped in the doorway, the sun low behind him. "Hey." He put his rifle on a side table. "You all right?"

She was now and threw herself into his arms. "Yeah." She couldn't get close enough, wanting to touch and smell him.

He kicked the door closed, locked it, and hugged her. "You're trembling. What happened?"

Too much adrenaline and relief was still racing through her at his return. "I'm horny. You were gone too long." She smacked his butt. "What happened out there?"

"Nothing. Nor will it. The guys are positioned at every spot where Victor's men might arrive, though I don't think they will. I scared them pretty damn bad."

An understatement. "Is your team as expert at shooting as you?"

"They are, and then some. Not that Victor's shit will go on much longer now."

The "now" threw her. "What do you mean?"

He eased back, elation dancing in his eyes like a kid at Christmas. "There's something I want you to see." He pulled her to a kitchen chair, sat, then settled her on his lap. "Comfortable?"

Sitting like this beat out everything else. She touched her nose to his. "Completely. Is this what you wanted to show me? If it is, I'm already enjoying myself."

He kissed her hard then pressed his cheek to hers. "Keep that thought. This involves another matter." With his arm wrapped around her waist, he leaned forward and pulled something from his back pocket.

The phone Victor's man had dropped.

Her expectation ticked up several notches. "Please tell me there's more than porn in there."

"You won't believe what I've found, and I haven't gone through the entire memory yet." He brought up a video, the "start" arrow slightly below Victor's face. His broad smile was creepy as shit and deepened the wrinkles on his cheeks and around his pale-blue eyes. He'd slicked back his salt-and-pepper hair and wore a silver-and-turquoise bolo tie, his white shirt spotless. "What is this?"

"Listen." Ghost started the video.

Victor laughed, an obnoxious, sniggering sound. "Yeah, we got them good, didn't we?"

In the background, male voices murmured approval, one rising above the others. "Bryce Caldwell ain't gonna give you trouble no more."

Her mouth went dry.

"That's right." Victor poured himself a whiskey and took a sip. "Best thing is, no one will ever know what really happened to my dearly departed neighbor."

"Just as you wanted, Boss." The same voice from before. "Your wire trick was pure genius. Quick. Easy. And deadly."

She gripped Ghost's leg.

Victor lowered his drink and glared to the side, presumably at the man. "You did remember to remove the wire, didn't you?"

"You bet, then threw it in the largest creek the next county over, exactly as you wanted."

His eyes narrowed. "Did anyone see you?"

"Don't know how they could. It was past midnight when I got there, not a light around or the moon, the surroundings darker than Caldwell's squaw and the bitch's mother."

The men laughed.

You lousy... Obscenities rose in Nic's throat. She forced them down, not wanting to miss a word.

"Good." Victor enjoyed his whiskey.

Another man spoke. "What now, Boss?"

"Lay low for a bit until this blows over. If Caldwell's absence doesn't get them to leave the state, which I believe it will, I have other plans."

"Such as?"

"More lawsuits, what else? The best way I know for them to blow through Caldwell's insurance money in a futile effort to protect themselves."

"What if that doesn't work? It hasn't yet."

"Then we'll fuck with their cattle." Victor chuckled. "I'd say it's about time for another so-called alien attack the law won't investigate."

"Why not eliminate the bitches?" Another man's voice. "Those stupid whores won't stand a prayer against us."

Victor tapped his forefinger against his glass. "We leave them for last. Draw this out. Make it pure torture. In no time at all, they'll run so fast from the land, we won't have a chance to wave goodbye."

Laughter and whistles erupted from the group.

When the noise quieted, another man spoke. "What if they refuse to leave on their own?"

"Then we help them along." He shrugged. "Accidents do happen. Like with poor Bryce." Victor's wide smile showed his gums. "As far as his lowlife family's concerned, no one will ever pin an unfortunate car accident or house fire on me. Not with Rettner and the judges in my pocket. I'm already drawing up plans for the property. No damn way is a darkie ever setting foot on that land again."

The video stopped.

Nausea, hope, then caution warred within her. She feared this might be a trick. "Why in the world would Victor want this recorded?"

"I doubt he knows it exists." Ghost put the phone on the table and rubbed her back. "My guess is the man who shot this doesn't trust Victor in the least. The video's insurance against *Boss* trying to pin Bryce's murder solely on the crew. Even though they carried it out, they could escape the death penalty by testifying against him. Everything Victor said proved he orchestrated the plan. That, alone, will get him a needle in the arm."

Nic preferred him wasting away in a cage. "What now? You can't turn the video over to Rettner. He'll destroy it. So will his deputies. No judge in this county will allow it either since Victor's words implicates them. If we take it somewhere else..." She'd seen too many *Law & Order* programs to believe this evidence would make it to a jury. A slick attorney would find some arcane statute claiming Victor's rights to privacy were more important than murder. Or would find a judge who agreed the evidence was too prejudicial to present, or illegally obtained, or whatever, ad nauseam. "We have to be careful."

Ghost gave her an odd look. "I wasn't planning on doing anything less."

"I mean with how we present this." An idea formed. Uncertain how crazy it might be, she pulled her computer over and brought up the page showing the militia and gang videos.

He looked at the screen. "What are you doing?"

"Finding a way to stop Victor from burying the video. We can't turn it over to law enforcement."

"There's no other choice."

"Sure there is." She gestured to the screen. "Remember seeing videos showing cops shooting African Americans in the back and vigilantes harassing people of color for using the pool at their own apartment complexes, or napping in a dorm at a college they attend, or simply breathing while being a minority? The videos were out before the law or perps could do anything to suppress them. The public took over, demanding justice. With the country—hell, the world—cheering the good guys on, for once those in power had to pay. There wasn't anywhere for them to hide or a reasonable way for them to explain away their behavior. Am I right?"

He hugged her fiercely. "You are. Let me make a call."

"To whom?"

"A person I know who's great with computers and can have the video posted for us. We don't want our names or IP addresses attached to this in any way. The information will come from an anonymous source…maybe the man who filmed this. I doubt he could wiggle out of that no matter how hard he tries to claim he didn't do so. My friend will make certain of it."

"Can he or she have my video from earlier play after Victor's and also add the pictures of the mutilated cattle? Those shots will prove his words—he intended to mess with the herd then Mom, Kanti, and me. It's practically a script."

"I don't see how that will be a problem. John's a whiz at this stuff."

Ghost made his call.

CHAPTER 8

THE VIDEO RAN on major internet sites and ones Nic didn't know existed. Within hours, it went viral and became the lead story on countless news channels. Talking heads discussed the terror Nic and her family had endured too long, each announcer appalled at how far Victor's racism had driven him.

The governor called for a special investigation and appointed a team to handle the matter.

Reporters shouted questions at Victor and his men as deputies from another county led them away in cuffs.

Victor's attorney insisted someone had set the man up. "The video's been doctored. We will prove it in court. Mr. Victor will be exonerated."

Rettner, his deputies, and numerous judges did the perp walk next, each proclaiming his innocence. Citizens who believed in them set up crowdfunding accounts to finance the legal defense until the sites shut them down.

The Klan and other supremacist groups promised to protest the initial court appearances and each one that followed, citing a statewide frame-up against the men.

On the days in question, no Klansman or other militant group showed up. A few towns-people did, carrying signs stating Montana was for real Americans. Tribal members carried banners to remind everyone they were the first citizens here and gladly welcomed diversity and fairness in *their* country.

News crews filmed the dissenting groups. The story died quickly, replaced by reports hinting at deals between the defendants and prosecutors. Being the cowards they were, Victor's men turned on him in a heartbeat, hoping to save their asses.

Weeks passed before the turmoil abated, Nic's mom and Kanti too afraid to leave the ranch, fearful someone in town might harm them.

It pained Nic to have brought more pain into

their lives. She'd foolishly believed Victor's words would prove what a monster he was and everyone would want him strung up. How wrong she was. "I shouldn't have suggested releasing the videos." She pressed her face against Ghost's shoulder and clung to him as a drowning person would. "I should have taken my chances with the law."

He kissed her forehead. "If you had, we might still be fighting Victor. Kanti's, your mom's, and your life would be in danger."

"Like now? You see the looks we get when we're in town."

"Looks can't kill. Plus, the protestors' average age is mid-sixties. Those fossils are dying off, taking their disgusting attitudes with them. No matter what some people say, the world is changing. They can't stop that, which is why they're running scared about losing their privilege and mouthing the shit they do. Never doubt you did the right thing. Things will die down when the next outrage hits the news."

A month after Victor's arrest, a respected executive in another state garnered reporters' and the public's attention. His wife and three young boys disappeared, their bodies later found in a wooded area near his mansion. He blamed the crime on his mistress, claiming she wouldn't leave him alone when he tried to end the relationship. She'd planted evidence on him at the burial site and in his house. She, in turn, claimed her husband's recent death wasn't an accident, but a plan by the executive to have her for his own. When she refused his advances, he killed his family to clear the way to having her.

The media gave their competing tales and accusations round-the-clock coverage.

However, Victor's story wasn't completely forgotten. TV newsmagazines contacted Nic about profiling the case on their programs. She turned them down. Tabloids offered staggering sums for her to give them an exclusive. She refused them, too, wanting nothing except an end to the madness and for everyone to leave them alone.

Little by little, peace settled in, until one afternoon in late fall.

The lead Deputy County Attorney arrived at the main house, asking to speak to Nic, her mom, and Kanti.

Nic had a sickening feeling, but showed the middle-aged woman in and introduced her.

Kanti wiped her hands on a dishtowel. "Can I get you anything to drink? Water? Coffee? Fruit juice?"

"Water would be fine, thank you." She smiled then glanced at Ghost who stood at Nic's side.

She held his hand. "He stays."

"Of course. Thank you." She accepted the water from Kanti.

Nic gestured the woman to a chair.

Everyone took their seats.

Unable to stand the suspense, Nic said the only thing she could. "Please don't tell me you're dropping the case against Victor."

"We're not." She put her glass on the end table and laced her fingers. "Mr. Victor's attorney contacted our office yesterday. His client wants to make a deal."

That didn't sound good. "What kind?"

"If we take the death penalty off the table, he'll plead guilty."

Nic's mom exchanged a glance with Kanti then spoke to the attorney. "Does that mean he'll eventually get out?"

"Not in the least. Our deal is life in prison without the possibility of parole. He'll die behind bars."

Sounded like a fair trade to Nic. However, she wanted more assurance. "In court, will he have to admit to what he did? How he had my grandfather murdered? Or does he simply plead guilty while maintaining his innocence—that he's been framed—and that's it?"

"What you're referring to is an Alford plea, where the defendant pleads guilty but doesn't admit to the crime. Unfortunately, this state does allow that. However, my office wants the plea tied to him admitting guilt in open court. His attorney's fighting us. That's why I'm here."

Ghost rested his forearms on his knees. "I'm not following."

Nic wasn't either. "Where's this leading?"

The attorney smoothed back her honey-blonde hair. "A trial will simply draw out the inevitable since we have more than enough evidence for the death penalty. I wanted to know what you and your family would like us to do. If you're good with life imprisonment without parole, we'll insist it's only on the table if Mr. Victor admits his guilt in court. If he doesn't, the death penalty is back on. His attorney knows he can't win this case. It's your choice as to how we proceed."

Nic looked at her mom and Kanti. "As long as he admits guilt and tells the world what he's done, I'm all for life without parole."

They nodded.

So did Ghost.

Tears stung Nic's eyes. As he'd promised the day they'd met, he'd helped her in immeasurable ways and had stood at her side throughout, eliminating the threat.

The trouble was finally over. Uncertainty, too.

Except for what would come next for her and Ghost...

EPILOGUE

THE FOLLOWING SPRING...

HAVING FINISHED his latest case for Brotherhood Protectors, Ghost gunned his pickup, not caring about the dust he stirred up on the rural road or the birds he'd startled.

He simply wanted to get home.

By the time the house was in view, sun lightened the horizon, turning the inky black a faint blue and rose.

As far as he was concerned, he wouldn't see the outside again for hours, possibly days. Before leaving his last assignment, he'd called Hank, requesting two weeks off.

"You got it." Hank's chair squeaked in the background. "In fact, take as much time as you want."

If that were the case, Ghost would leave the agency to become a rancher. A notion that kept nagging him.

Parked near the front steps, he hurried across the porch and opened the guesthouse door.

Shadows greeted him. As softly as he could, he closed and locked the door, lowered his knapsack, then shed his boots and clothes.

Naked, he padded to the bed and curled up behind Nic, her softness and heat snatching his breath.

"Ghost?" Sleep thickened her voice.

He nuzzled her neck. "Who else?"

She laughed softly. "I didn't expect you until noon."

He cupped her belly, their child growing inside. At week's end, they'd visit the OB-GYN for an ultrasound to learn the sex. Whether it was a boy or girl didn't matter to him as long as the child was healthy, happy, and loved.

He'd die for his family and his wife. He lifted Nic's hand and kissed the wedding ring he'd slipped on her finger at their ceremony on the reservation. "I couldn't stay away any longer. Do you mind?"

"Are you kidding?" She rolled over to face him, her eyes sparkling in the available light. "If I had my way, I'd tie you to our bed and would never let you leave."

"There's an idea. How about we start with two weeks? Hank promised not to phone, text, or email me during that time."

"He's a good man." She snuggled closer. "But you're better. Any ideas on what you'd like to do during your vacation?"

"Ours." He flexed his rigid cock against her thigh. "I have some thoughts...about other stuff, too."

"Yeah?" She rubbed her nose against his then pecked his lips. "You'd like to try spanking now? Maybe a little BDSM? Voyeurism? A fetish or—"

"Ranching."

"Two— What?"

He was reluctant to repeat himself, but each time he left her side for extended periods, his heart took too hard a beating. He'd searched his entire life for her and didn't want to waste even a minute between them. "Don't get me wrong, I love working for the Brotherhood. But I'm tired of going on the road. With the little one coming, I'd like to be around when she or he says that first word, takes a step, gets a tooth, pitches a fit."

"You mean it?"

"About the fit?"

"No." She smacked his ass playfully. "About staying here all the time."

"Since you already know I'm a lousy liar, what do you think?"

She searched his face. "That you might be doing this for me?"

"Not even close. I'm being selfish. I don't want to be away from you. Hell, I'd like to be underfoot every damn day. Would you mind?"

"Seriously?" She hugged him. "Why do you think Kanti and my mom have been plying you with their best meals and asking you to make decisions around the ranch? They've been grooming you to stay put. So have I."

"You? In what way?"

"The one I like best." She rested his hand on her pussy. "I have to be honest, though. Making love three times every night with quickies between chores is kind of exhausting."

Their schedule had practically killed him. Not that he'd ever complain. Still... "You mean we're going to cut down to only twice a night and nothing in the afternoon?"

"Not anytime soon, unless you want to piss me off." She kissed him deep, hard, and long then pulled her mouth free, her lips wet from his. "With my hormone levels, crossing me isn't wise."

He brought her face back to his. "Wouldn't think of it. There's no place I'd rather be than beside or inside you."

"Yeah? Prove it."

He eased her closer and did. His love for her and this land deepened further, their bond unbreakable no matter what the future held.

Paranormal Dating Agency

<u>My Book</u>

Muzzling the Beast

Book Four – Taming the Beast

<u>https://amzn.to/2MxeMeH</u>

Thrust Into Danger

The Phoenix Agency

<u>https://amzn.to/2Mqanyp</u>

Death Sentence

Omega Team

<u>https://amzn.to/2Pl8MHD</u>

Adored

<u>https://bit.ly/2mtOiiH</u>

Wicked Design

Book Four – Wicked Brand

<u>https://amzn.to/2xFXZ6q</u>

SiNN

https://amzn.to/2sLifhT

Mastering the Beast

Book Three – Taming the Beast

https://amzn.to/2I2NuPi

Surrendering to the Beast

Book Two – Taming the Beast

https://amzn.to/2JiYPaW

Wicked Times Two

Book Three – Wicked Brand

http://amzn.to/2ohAB7k

Forbidden Desire

Book Three – Pirate's Prize

http://amzn.to/2GmOf0i

Wicked Seduction

Book Two – Wicked Brand

http://amzn.to/2zeN6b4

Sinfully Wicked

Book One – Wicked

http://amzn.to/2wSgfs9

Freeing the Beast

Book One – Taming the Beast

http://amzn.to/2ECK6c8

Return to Ecstasy

Book One – Her Master's Pleasure

http://amzn.to/2t4YDmQ

Wicked Takeover

Book One – Wicked Brand

http://amzn.to/2uvMxqM

Days of Desire

Book Two – Pirate's Prize

http://amzn.to/2EPQeNp

First Comes Desire

Book One – Pirate's Prize

http://amzn.to/2fRpdd1

Destined for Each Other

http://amzn.to/2kdMNX9

Passionate Pursuit

Book Three – Dangerous Desires

http://amzn.to/2qqwp4k

Wicked Whispers

Book Two – Dangerous Desires

http://amzn.to/2qgnCFE

Moonlight Danger

Hot Moon Rising Series

http://amzn.to/2oJtuas

Pleasure Me

Black Hills Wolves Series

http://amzn.to/2qgEXhG

Loving Lies

Book One – Dangerous Desires

http://amzn.to/2pgQBrM

Got Muscle?

Men for Hire Anthology

http://amzn.to/2qiWxyO

Intimate Details

http://amzn.to/2qiZqj6

This Time When We Touch

http://amzn.to/2pw50kf

ABOUT TINA DONAHUE

Tina is an Amazon and international bestselling novelist who writes passionate romance for every taste—"heat with heart"—for traditional publishers and indie. *Booklist, Publisher's Weekly, Romantic Times* and numerous online sites have praised her work. She's won Readers' Choice Awards, was named a finalist in the EPIC competition, received a Book of the Year award, The Golden Nib Award, awards of merit in the RWA Holt Medallion competitions, and second place in the NEC RWA contests. She's featured in the Novel & Short Story Writer's Market. Before penning romances, she worked at a major Hollywood production company in Story Direction.

On a less serious note: She's an admitted and unrepentant chocoholic, brakes for Mexican restaurants, and has been known to moan like Meg Ryan in *When Harry Met Sally* while wolfing down tostadas. She's flown a single-engine airplane (freaking scary), rewired an old house using an 'electricity for dummies' book, and is horribly shy despite the hot romances she writes.

Learn more about Tina and her novels here:

FB Fanpage:

https://www.facebook.com/DonahueTina1/

Website/Blog:

http://tinadonahuebooks.blogspot.com/

Newsletter:

http://tinadonahuebooks.blogspot.com/p/newsletter.html

BookBub:

http://bit.ly/2phWWDu

Instagram:

https://www.instagram.com/tinadonahuebooks/

Goodreads:

http://bit.ly/1wFmIu6

Twitter:

http://bit.ly/1ziy4IU

Facebook:

http://on.fb.me/1Dl8DHy

Triberr:

http://bit.ly/1CE2ec7

Pinterest:

http://bit.ly/1yFLeMx

Amazon author page:

http://amzn.to/1ChWFkO

TRR:

http://bit.ly/1vb7eEc

Sweet 'n Sexy Divas:

http://bit.ly/1ChWN3K

Romance Books 4 US:

http://bit.ly/1JPtfeS

facebook.com/DonahueTina1

instagram.com/tinadonahuebooks

ORIGINAL BROTHERHOOD
PROTECTORS SERIES

BY ELLE JAMES

ABOUT ELLE JAMES

ELLE JAMES also writing as MYLA JACKSON is a *New York Times* and *USA Today* Bestselling author of books including cowboys, intrigues and paranormal adventures that keep her readers on the edges of their seats. With over eighty works in a variety of sub-genres and lengths she has published with Harlequin, Samhain, Ellora's Cave, Kensington, Cleis Press, and Avon. When she's not at her computer, she's traveling, snow skiing, boating, or riding her ATV, dreaming up new stories. Learn more about Elle James at www.ellejames.com

Website | Facebook | Twitter | GoodReads |
Newsletter | BookBub | Amazon

Follow Elle!
www.ellejames.com
ellejames@ellejames.com